Sadie
and the Silver Shoes

illustrated by

Jane Godwin   Anna Walker

CANDLEWICK PRESS

For Anna
I'm so glad we found each other.
J. G.

For dear Meg
A. W.

First U.S. edition 2019
First published by Penguin Random House Australia 2018

Library of Congress Catalog Card Number pending
ISBN 978-1-5362-0480-3

CCP 24 23 22 21 20 19
10 9 8 7 6 5 4 3 2 1

Printed in Shenzhen, Guangdong, China

This book was typeset in Gill Sans.
The illustrations were done in watercolor and collage.

Candlewick Press
99 Dover Street
Somerville, Massachusetts 02144

visit us at www.candlewick.com

Sadie had three brothers:
Walter, Max, and Finn.

When Walter's clothes were too
small for him, they went to Max.

When they were too small
for Max, they went to Finn.

And when they were too small
for Finn, they went to Sadie.

Sadie didn't mind,

but some people did.
Like Annabelle, at school.

The only clothes Sadie got to pick
were underwear and shoes.
That's why Sadie loved shoes.
New shoes.

And one day, Sadie saw
the most beautiful shoes ever. . . .

Sadie wore her new
silver shoes everywhere.

"These are absolutely my most
favorite shoes," she said.
"See how they sparkle in the sun?"

Her mom had even gotten them
a bit big so they would last longer.

Sadie put them on when they
went for a picnic that weekend.

"They'll get dirty..."
said Mom.

"I'm going on an adventure,"
said Walter.

"Me too," said Max.

"Me too," said Finn.

"Yes, yes, let's go!" said Sadie.

It was a good adventure.

Until . . .

Oh, no!

Sadie scrambled,

Walter stumbled,

Max slipped,

and Finn fell in.

They all got very wet . . .

but they didn't catch the shoe.

It was swept down the creek
like a shimmering silver fish.

"Maybe you should have worn
old shoes today," said Mom.

"I know!" shouted Sadie.
"I know that *now*!"

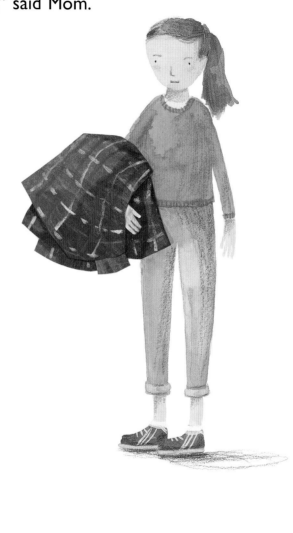

And she marched off in a very angry mood.

What could Sadie do with her one left shoe?

"You could plant a flower in it,"
suggested Walter.

"Could it hold your pencils?"
asked Max.

"Hang it from your window,
like a mobile!" said Finn.

Sadie loved her one shoe so much,
she decided she would wear it anyway.

"Your shoes don't match,"
said Annabelle.

"I don't care," said Sadie.

At school, the teacher made an announcement.

"Next Monday, a new girl is coming.
Sadie, would you like to
show her around?"

What would the new girl be like?
Sadie wondered.

The new girl's name was Ellie.
Sadie showed her around.

But Ellie wasn't looking at the playground,
or the library, or the cafeteria.

Ellie was looking at Sadie's shoe.
Was she going to say it didn't match?
Was she going to go play with Annabelle?

"I have a shoe like that," said Ellie.

"Really? Just one shoe?" said Sadie.
"Is it a right or a left shoe?"

"I'm not sure," said Ellie. "Come to my house
after school and we can look."

At Ellie's house, Sadie looked.
She looked closer. Could it be . . . ?

It wasn't as shiny, but . . .

"This is my shoe!" said Sadie.
"My other absolutely most favorite shoe!"

"I found it at the beach
 near my old house," said Ellie.
"I thought it was a fish with shiny scales.
 Mom said that one shoe is useless,
 but I still kept it."

They put the shoes together on the bed.

"I'm glad I did," said Ellie.
"Would you like it back?"

Sadie thought for a moment.

"Does it fit you?" she asked.

"Yes," said Ellie.

And from that day on,
Sadie and Ellie wore their most favorite shoes everywhere.

Sometimes Sadie wore them,
sometimes Ellie wore them,
and sometimes they wore one each.